The Greatest Illusion

The Greatest Illusion

Ashley Rose

authorHOUSE®

AuthorHouse™
1663 Liberty Drive
Bloomington, IN 47403
www.authorhouse.com
Phone: 1-800-839-8640

Published by AuthorHouse   04/28/2012

ISBN: 978-1-4772-0213-5 (sc)
ISBN: 978-1-4772-0214-2 (e)

Library of Congress Control Number: 2012907788

Contents

Chapter One

One deep breath after another, one step at a time. The doctors will always tell you that. They will tell you grief fades if I just move forward. No one understands my situation especially since I'm twenty three years of age and have no job. My parents divorced when I was still a child so I never really knew the love of a father, just my mother. I guess I had a pretty normal life. I've had my struggles, my tears, and those moments where I questioned my very existence, but who hasn't?

My mother, Lillian Auditore, came from a small village in Italy when she was very young. She learned English quickly. Even then she was afraid of not being accepted by the people around her. I'm a spitting image of her. We both have wavy light brown hair, light brown eyes, light, almost tan skin, and we're both short with a little chub, as I call it. She recently got married to some Greek man when she went on vacation. It was then that I realized I needed to move on with my life.

My ex-boyfriend, Chris, helped me realize I needed to get away from this small town. He was, well, how do you explain this? — He was insane — No, that's not right. He was a good boyfriend that I met during high school. I've always seen the best in people and that always got me hurt. He tried to kill me because he thought I was flirting with everyone at my job at Star Bucks. I quit just for him but I ran off anyway. I'm now in a bigger town, almost a city looking for a job and an apartment.

It's mid October and it's already cold. I pull on my jacket and keep walking down the sidewalk, through the fallen, withered leaves on the ground. This town reminds me of San Francisco. The buildings are all seemingly conjoined and look Victorian. The street is modern at least. I stop at a vacant white marble hotel that stands out due to the two large pillars that guard a revolving door.

I smile as the light bulb in my head turns on. I could re-open this hotel, live in it and make it my own. Perfect. I clap my hands and rush inside.

My heart seemingly stops beating and my jaw drops.

It's an up and running hotel but I could have sworn it was vacant. Maybe I'm insane because it also looks straight from the early nineteenth century or the late eighteenth century. Green, floral wallpaper cover the walls, there is one check in counter that looks more like a desk. A grand, oak wood staircase stands fifteen feet from where I stand. Red, velvet Victorian couches are on either side of the staircase. On one couch, people in modern clothes sit, on the other, people in Victorian clothing sit. To the left there are big, open French doors that lead to a theater, I think. An elevator sits on the right. The doors open and an actual elevator helper man is in there, in the clothing they wore in the past. Round hat and everything.

"May I help you miss?" A sudden voice comes from beside me making me jump.

I turn to see a bell hop in the old clothes.

"Miss, are you all right? Do you need a room?" He says. I read his golden tag that reads "Raul".

I shake my head. "I, uh, need a job . . . ."

3

Raul's eyes widen. "Are you sure?"

"I think. I could have sworn this place was vacant, but I was mistaken."

"Right this way, miss." He leads me to the desk. At my entrance, a man in a suit comes up with a big smile. He's kind of heavy for a tall guy.

"Good evening, madam. I am Demetrius, how may I assist you?" He says very perky.

"She wants a job." Raul says shakily, as if frightened.

Demetrius' smile turns into a straight line. "Well, what brings you here?"

I shrug, not wanting to give my life story. "My name is Alessandra Auditore. I thought this building was vacant, but since it isn't, is there any positions available?"

At that moment, a girl screams and runs out of the building.

Demetrius and Raul laugh in unison.

"Do you have a strong stomach?" Demetrius asks.

"Are you frightened easily?" Raul asks.

I tilt my head in confusion. "Yes and no."

"Well, come with me, darling." Demetrius comes around the desk and hooks his arm with mine. "Let me escort you to Catalin. He's not only the owner of this fine hotel, but also the greatest magician ever."

"I never heard of him. I've heard of Harry Houdini, Siegfried and Roy, Criss Angel, and yeah." I say.

Demetrius laughs his hearty, husky laugh again. "Oh, you're in for a surprise, Miss Auditore." He leads me to the theater where I see a faint figure of a man sitting on the stage. I think he has his head bowed, I cannot tell with the dim lighting.

Demetrius clears his throat as we approach him. He releases my arm and claps his hands twice and the theater grows brighter and the man is in clear sight. "Sir, Catalin, I have you a new assistant."

The man, Catalin, raises his head.

Oh. My. Goddess. He's gorgeous! His black hair is tied back, his pale skin makes his crystal blue eyes pop. He hops off the stage and levels up to Demetrius. He wears black sweats and a white T-shirt.

"A little forewarning would have been nice." Catalin snaps. "I do not need another woman to come here, waste my time, and run off like a boy in war!"

His yell echoes through the theater.

"Pardon me, sir." I say, surprising them both. "I need this job. I need a sanctuary. I have always had an interest with magic. If you don't mind, can you please give me a chance?"

Catalin looks into my eyes and pulls me into a trance. He breaks it by looking down. "Very well. Demetrius, show her to her room where she'll stay. We'll start in the morning." He turns and walks to and through a back door.

ଽଠChapter Two‍ଓ୪

It takes me ten minutes to adapt to the beautiful room.
A bay window is the focal point of the room. A white
lounge chair sits in the middle of the window with a
matching ottoman. The ivory and baby pink floral wall
paper compliments the fluffy white carpet. The bed!
A huge bed that looks so comfortable but that could
just be the fluffy light pink comforter and matching
pillows. I walk toward the bay window and discover
that there's more to the room. A little piano is on one
side and a vanity and a brown armoire on the other.

I nod with a smile. I think I'll be quite happy here.
I just need to get my stuff.

"Okay . . . ." I say to myself. "Where's a phone?"

"Oh, there is no such thing, silly!" A light female voice comes from behind me.

I turn and shriek at the sudden sight of pale, almost see-through woman. She's beautiful but is she alive? I take in the sight of her. Her blond hair has been bobbed and she is dressed in a nice emerald dress with a green silk bow tied around her waste that match her green eyes. The dress scoops down to her chest, but a white lace something covers anything that would have been shown.

"Well, good evening, darling. I'm Melina." She says with a smile and a slight Southern accent. "This was my room before—Uh. Never mind that thought. What's your name?"

"Alessandra." I take in everything. "Before what exactly, Melina?"

She shakes her head, her hair staying almost glued to her slim, perfect face. "Don't mind that thought. You are the new assistant. Have fun. Want me to help you prepare for it?"

"No, thank you. I just need to make a phone call."

She gives me a nonplussed look. "To whom, Alessandra?"

I close my eyes and draw in a sharp breath at the sudden realization of my reality. My mother has moved on, Chris moved on. That's why I'm here, so I can move on as well.

"Melina," I say, smiling suddenly. "Ready to help me?"

"Of course!"

I soon find out that Melina is in love with that little piano. Ever since five o'clock, she's been playing various pieces, from Mozart to Beethoven and random people. Now, seven hours later, she is still going. I hope I'm as amazing as she is when I die.

A sudden knock on the door makes me jolt up and Melina stops playing. A mask of fear has replaced her normally calm and happy face. At the second knock and the clearing of a throat, Melina disappears.

"Who is it?" I ask, walking over to the door.

"Catalin, please, open up." He says. I go to check the peep hole, but I only bump my head on the door since there is no peep hole.

"Opening!" I say, opening the door. The sight of him takes my breath away. His hair is no longer tied back and it's damp and dangles just shy above his broad shoulders. He is now wearing jeans and a light blue button up shirt that hangs loose.

He smiles, showing Hollywood perfect white and straight teeth. "I see you've met Melina. She is quite a character."

I nod, afraid to say anything.

He catches on to my anxiety and his smile fades. "Have you eaten today?"

I take that question in and try to remember when I last ate and what.

Oh, yeah, I had a piece of cherry pie this morning.

"I last ate breakfast." I say quietly. "At least I ate something."

Catalin looks down for a second. "Where are my manners? I should have asked you to dinner with me."

"Oh, it's okay! I'm kind of tired anyway. I rather sleep."

"Nonsense. I'll have something brought up for you. I will see you in the morning."

"Yeah, definitely. Thank you again."

"Good night and I am not sure if Demetrius told you this but you must be in your room before eleven." He turns away before I can reply.

I close the door slowly and take a deep breath and exhale.

"Is he gone?" Melina whispers, reappearing before me.

"He just left." I half laugh. "Are you afraid of him?"

She gasps, dramatically placing her hand over her mouth. "He is the master. You mustn't cross him. That's why I avoid him at all costs."

"Master? Melina, this is the twentieth century or twenty first, or whatever. There is — are — no masters. Wait, what era are you from?"

Melina steps back. "I must go." She disappears without answering my question.

❧Chapter Three☙

I wake up in the morning. I have no idea what the time is, but judging by how the sun is coming in through the window, it must be before noon. I check my cell phone which has completely died now. I check the little round clock on my night stand. It is eight o'clock on the dot or line.

I dress in sweats and a T-shirt and head out the door. I feel very un-proper as I walk down the dim hallway and pass elegantly dressed guests. I tie my hair back as I head to the elevator.

"Good morning, Miss Auditore." The elevator operator says, bowing slightly.

"Please, call me Alessa." I say, stepping into the elevator. I read his gold name tag to find his name is a French name, I think. "Adolphe is it?"

"Indeed. You have no reason to call me by name, miss." He pulls the lever down to the section that reads LOBBY. Down we go.

I rush to the theater only to find it dark and vacant. I gasp as a hand grasps my shoulder. I turn and try to see but it's too dark. The hand slides down my arm and to my hand. Without a word, I am led out of the dark theater and back to the lobby. I smile to see Catalin.

"I don't start that early." Catalin says with a faint smile. "You must eat first."

I remember my huge dinner. "I think I'm still full from last night." I look at his outfit which resembles mine. "Hey, we match!" I say, laughing, making him laugh.

"You, my darling, are quite a catch. Come along." I follow him down a corridor and into a grand dining hall that resembles the one Rose in the *Titanic* sat at. I am at a loss for words and I stand there, jaw dropped, looking around the room.

"You are blocking the door, child." An elderly woman says, tapping on my upper arm.

"Sorry, I'm new." I say awkwardly, looking for Catalin now.

"I can tell."

"Excuse me." I rush off and look for a bar of some sort that you usually see in hotels that you can serve yourself. I don't find one, but I find Catalin sitting by himself, looking at me and trying hard not to laugh.

"Sit, please." He says sternly.

"Yes, master." I say with a high pitch tone that I always used on my mother. I sit on the chair opposite of him. "Where's the food bar."

"You do not serve yourself here." He says just as a waiter approaches with two covered trays that only look small but there is so much under them. I learned that last night. "Don't call me master."

"My bad."

"Here you are." The waiter says, gingerly placing our trays down. He is an older black man who looks as nervous as Tom being chased by the bull dog. "Eggs Benedict with ham and Belgium waffles."

"Thank you very much." I say with a smile, making him calm down.

Catalin clears his throat and the waiter goes back to the nervous stance.

"Sir, is there a problem?" The waiter says.

"Where is the maple?" Catalin says softly.

"I will get that right away."

"I don't need any so you don't need to get a big thing." I try to chime in but it goes unheard for he rushes off. I glance at Catalin. What is going on here?

We eat in silence. I feel his gaze on me, but I do not dare look back. Once we finish, I naturally start gathering the dishes and utensils.

"I can get that, Miss Auditore. But thank you." The waiter says, taking the plates from me.

"Thank you." I say as he walks off.

"Come." Catalin orders, heading back through the dining hall. I leave a tip on the table out of habit and follow after my new master.

"Again!" Catalin orders. I had no idea that in order to be an assistant, I had to be in shape. For the past couple of hours, Catalin had me running around the theater, lifting crates, etcetera. After that single word, I drop down to the floor. My chest heaves up and down as I try to catch my breath. My hair that has escaped the hair tie is stuck to my sweat-covered face. I wish I knew I had to be in shape. I feel my breakfast in my throat and swallow hard.

"Five minutes, please." I whines.

"Get up." Catalin orders and I hear him walk over. "Now!"

At that, I sit up and look at him. His eyes are no longer blue but now a dark, deep green.

"Please. Just five minutes." I repeat.

"Fine. Do as you please." He turns away. For almost no reason at all, I start crying hard, almost bawling.

I tie my hair back up and stand up. My legs tremble, but I force myself to do it. "I'm sorry."

"Are you finished?" He says, sitting on a random velvet chair.

"Again?"

He nods. I take a deep breath and start running again. If this doesn't kill me, well, I might be Super Girl.

After two more laps, Catalin stops me. His eyes are still that dark green. He stands up, sending chills down my spine.

"Promise me you'll be better tomorrow. You are not a child and I will not allow you to act like one." He snaps.

"I promise." I say, biting my lip back.

"On to the act." He walks past me and makes his way to the stage. I turn around and face the stage.

Catalin lends me his hand and I take it and let him pull me up. "I will have you know there are no tricks. There are no trap doors. I have mastered everything."

"Criss Angel doesn't do that either. Well, he has cameras." I say.

"He's a fool. Do not mention him."

"That was the last time."

"Good." He smiles. "Don!"

At that, a scrawny, almost a teenage boy scurries to Catalin, holding a cage with two doves in it. Catalin takes the cage and the boy, Don, runs off.

"Here, would you like to hold one?" Catalin says, opening the small door. He pulls the smaller dove out. "This is the female, Juliet."

"She's beautiful." I say, taking the dainty creature in my hands. I look into Catalin's eyes which have gone back to the comforting blue.

"This is Romeo." He says, taking the male out and sets the cage down. "Funny, Juliet hates being handled but she seems to like you."

I bring Juliet close to my face. A sweet look of innocence is within her black eyes.

❦Chapter Four❧

I walk down a dark hallway. I see a distant light. I know it is early yet in the morning. A scorching four o'clock a.m. and it burns my flesh but I cannot close my eyes which is the very key to ending the pain. I keep walking, yearning to reach the light. The show — my first show, the one that no one surpasses — is tonight.

Breathing in the memories of my past, each step I take toward the light represent how much I'm willing to move on.

I'm stopped abruptly by a silhouette of man. He blocks the end of the hall with his tall, bulky figure. I take another step and discover the man to be Catalin. He bows his head slightly.

It's time for the preparation.

"You look beautiful, Miss Auditore." Don says shakily as I step from my dressing room.

"Do I?" I ask childishly. "Where is a mirror?"

Don smiles and tries to refrain from a giggle. "Follow me!" He leads me through the sea of thick, velvet curtains until we reach a full length mirror with a halo of white light bulbs around it. I stare at my reflection and almost faint. I look so different. Make-up took over and changed my face. My costume is so revealing, I feel the need to wear a floor-length robe. The gold sequin bra top covers just my breasts and a matching floor-length skirt slits all the way up my left leg, revealing my black shorts underneath and my gold two inch heels.

"Damn, I look like a hooker!" I say with a twitch of my upper lip.

Don starts rolling on the floor, giggling.

"Enough, Don." Catalin says from behind.

Don's eyes start to tear and he scampers off back into the sea of curtains.

Catalin smiles and extends his hand. "Come, Alessa."

I take his hand and follow him to the opening of the stage. The mixture of sounds coming from the full theater make me tremble. The talking, the laughing, the coughing, everything.

I take a deep breath. "Now." When I don't get a reply, I know that Catalin has turned away and that I should step toward the crate that awaits my fate. I step onto the stage and remember the mask over my face, it's already smiling for me.

"Good evening, ladies and gentlemen!" I say loudly over the crowd.

The crowd throws an applause and whistles at me.

"Are you ready for what you are about to witness?" I say softly as the crowd silences. "Beware, your mind will never be the same."

"It already isn't!" Someone calls out from the crowd, making my smile stumble in unison with my step.

I motion toward the giant crate that sits over a bottomless table to show there are no tricks. Now I think about how this is going to work out.

"Metamorphis!" I snap, causing the crowd to gasp. "One second here, the next gone. Is it illusion? Is it a trick? Or could it be that you saw something wrong?"

Mumbles float into the air.

I place my right index finger over my pressed lips, silencing the crowd. "Something lurks within this crate . . . ." I knock twice on the crate, listening in for the cue. When I hear the faint tap, I open the crate and Catalin jumps out with a sudden burst of flame. He squats on the floor, smiling wickedly at the crowd. It's then I notice his eyes are that dark green. The crowd is a mixture of screams and cheers and giggles. Catalin stands up and paces the stage slowly, locking eyes with various strangers.

He does a series of various acts where I mostly rush back stage and retrieve things from Don and bring them back to Catalin.

It isn't until fifteen minutes later that I'm to come in. I hold out a Japanese paper fan and wave it as Catalin rips up a single piece of paper. He tilts his head slightly to the right where I stand, cueing me to wave the fan faster. I do so and he lets the slivers of the paper dance gracefully over the fan, slowing disappearing as they hit the fan.

The crowd gasps and I can't help but to chuckle. I know this trick. I do not know how to do it myself, but Catalin makes it seems so simple.

I jump as he snatches the fan from me. "She stole it!"

I dramatically place my hand over my heart. "I was only trying to help!" I dramatically stomp off the stage, down the stairs and toward the crowd. A spotlight follows me and hovers over me.

"My love, come back!" Catalin yells, falling to his knees. The crowd laughs.

"Never!" I keep walking up the aisle, professionally ignoring all the butt slaps and crude comments. I turn slowly toward the stage. Catalin rises and starts waving the fan and as if on rewind, the slivers of paper start flying upward and come back together and form a whole piece of paper again.

Catalin kisses the paper and crumples it up and tosses it into the crowd. He bows as the crowd applauses.

Now, as I practiced, I run in my heels back to the stage. I jump into Catalin's arms and he swings me around. It's just as we had practiced, but this moment feels so intimate, I almost wish to stay in his arms.

He releases me and faces the crowd. "Now for the main event. Alessa, are you ready?"

"Of course, Master!" I say jokingly, making the crowd laugh.

Catalin shoots me a sarcastic cold glare. "Don!"

The small boy rushes from behind the curtain and gets on all fours by the table. I lift the lid off the crate as Catalin steps onto Don's back and gets into the crate. Catalin pulls the blue velvet sack over his head and sits in the crate. I tie the sack tight, as ordered. Don rushes back stage and returns with the chains and locks. I wrap a chain around the tie of the sack and lock it. I put the lid back on the crate and lock it up. A stage man I never met lifts me on to the top of the crate.

"I need your help, my loves." I say softly. "Please . . . . Count down from ten."

"Ten! . . . Nine! . . . Eight! . . . Seven! . . . Six! . . . Five! . . . Four! . . . Three! . . . Two! . . . ONE!" The crowd counts anxiously and just as they scream one, the air in my lungs seem to escape and the world goes dark. Claustrophobia takes over as I find myself in the sack. I pull on the edges, fear taking over. I feel sweat droplets slide down my face and they soak the sack as I try to get out. I hear the crowd cheer faintly. I hear the lid pop open and someone fumbles with the chains that contain me in here. Soon, I'm lifted out of the crate. Unable to stand on my own two feet, I fall to the floor and fight for my breath. Romeo and Juliet soar through the air and fly backstage. I frantically look for Catalin and cannot find him. Did something go wrong?

I try to lift myself up, but I fall back down and heave for a breath. The crowd doesn't seem to care or even notice. I see them all standing and facing the back of the theater as Catalin makes his way down, not toward me, but to the lobby. I start to cry softly, but quickly get over it. I pass out soon.

When I awake, someone is calling my name and the theater is vacant.

"Miss Auditore, are you okay? Do I need to fetch a doctor?" I hear Don say.

I roll over and face the boy. "I'm all right. I guess I'll need to get used to it."

He nods and giggles. "Trust me. You'll have to get used to no one caring."

I shrug. "I guess I already am. How'd it look?"

"Stunning. You vanished into thin air."

"Up, up!" I hear a feminine voice call from behind Don. "Watch out. Alessandra, you were grand!"

I awkwardly rise back to my feet and almost lose my breath again at the sight of the stunning woman before me. Her blond hair curls and just avoids her elbows. Her fair skin goes well with her white with silver tinted satin dress that V's down her chest and up her right leg. Her light green eyes sparkle with the theater lights.

"I'm Lucille." She says with a graceful tone of a proper lady. "I am the singer of this joint. You did wonderful. Most girls run off either during practices or during the fan act."

"Well, thanks a lot. Will I get to see you perform?" I ask.

She laughs. "Of course! I perform tomorrow. Let's go get food. With me, my love, you will eat the greatest food ever!"

Lucielle starts off the stage.

"Come on, Don." I say, reaching for the boy.

He shakes his head. "I ain't allowed to, miss. I get the scraps."

"Nonsense! Come on." I plead, stepping toward him.

"Alessandra, there is much for you to learn. Refrain from foolishness." A stern voice comes from the theater door. Catalin. Anger boils in my blood for a ripple of a second. I roll my eyes and walk toward him. He locks his arm with mine and leads me to the crowd. I am asked silly questions and match them with silly answers. I make small talk but I make absolutely nothing out.

After an hour, Catalin leads me past the elevator and toward the dining hall, but I stop him and step back.

"I don't want to go. Can I please eat in my room?" I ask nervously.

Catalin looks at me with his eyes still green. "We had a wonderful show."

"My ass." I snap, surprising myself. "Sorry. I . . . . I just need to get used to this. But I can't start off so quick. Please understand. That's all I'm asking of you."

"As you wish." He turns and walks all the way toward the hall.

"That little —" Lucielle growls, coming beside me. "Come with me." She takes my hand and leads me into the dining hall. All heads turn toward me and laughter fills the room.

"Damn it, Lucille!" I choke out.

The laughter grows louder and I snap when I see Catalin laughing. I turn around and run to the emergency stairs and run down and down the endless flights of stairs until I reach the darkened bottom. I open the door and curiously walk down the cold and damp corridor. I see a single light coming from the right side of the hall. I walk into that room in the corner of my eye, I see a swimming pool. Something makes me stop but I walk all the way in anyway. The swimming pool is still. I look inside and then at my swollen ankles. It is almost too tempting to let the poisoned water eat my shoes.

I sink to the cool concrete floor and almost place my feet in the icy water when I hear a sudden groan.

"This place is like no other." A deep manly voice comes from the corner of the giant room. Soon, a slim Hispanic man steps toward me. He is dressed in ripped jeans, ragged work boots and a dirty white shirt. His long black hair almost covers his round face.

"I first came here a couple years ago and haven't been able to leave since." He says softly, sitting beside me. "I got so confused by everything I saw. I went home, was so distracted, I almost got killed at work. So I came back. I can't afford a room, so I stay down here. I saw you perform though. You shouldn't have been laughed at. But they always laugh at the new people."

"Why?" I breathe out. "Just why?"

"Simple." He says. "They expect you to be gone. They don't know you're down here. They think you left. Go back up. It ain't worth crying over."

"Not yet. Not yet . . ."

"Don't you dare step a pinky toe in that damned water."

Later that night, as I sit in my room, I wonder if this will change if I simply stay. I am so ready to prove these crazy folks wrong.

❧ Chapter Five ☙

For the following weeks, I work harder beyond my limit. In the process, I've sprained my ankle and both my wrists. I didn't let it stop me. Catalin has no idea what to think of me. Don has stuck by me because unfortunately, I'm the only one nice to him. All the shows have been successful due to my help.

A month and a half have gone by without a single thank you. But Christmas is right around the corner. Maybe these concrete angels could use some holiday spirit.

"A *Christmas* tree in *my* lobby?!" Demetrius yells at my idea. I just poured my ideas into his empty glass that maybe once was filled with happiness.

I nod with a cheesy smile. I nudge him with my elbow. "Come on, old sport!"

He holds back a laugh. "When Catalin leaves for the evening . . . . But don't say a word and I will tell him it was all you."

I cheer and wrap my arms around him. "Thank you!" I step back as he grunts.

"No, thank you." He pats my hand. "Here he comes."

I turn toward the grand staircase where Catalin descends in elegance. He walks over to Demetrius without a single glance at me.

"Good evening, sir." Demetrius says.

Catalin bows his head. "I have to meet with this amazing magician."

"Just look in the mirror." I say softly. But when I get a weird gaze in return, I regret the comment.

"Anyway," Catalin says, "I shall be back right before the show. Alessa knows what to do if I happen to be behind schedule." At that, Catalin makes his exit.

"Let's do this." Demetrius says.

Lucille, Demetrius, Don and I take a step back and smile in approval at our work at redecorating the lobby. Snakes of gold, red, and green tinsel wrap around the walls. A giant Christmas tree sits in the corner right by the door, dressed in silver tinsel, white lights and various dark blue, red, green, and yellow ornaments. On top, a porcelain angel dressed in red smiles down at everyone. A green blanket is wrapped around the trunk to catch fallen pines. The doorknobs have snowflake stickers on them.

A couple of guests walk in and smile wide at the site of the lobby.

More guests arrive.

"The show!" I gasp and rush to the theater which is already starting to fill. I run backstage and practically dive into my costume and make-up. It takes me a minute to run the show over in my head. Catalin will be late and I have to amuse the crowd.

I run on to the stage and purposely trip, stumble, but stand straight up. To my luck, laughter is my reward.

"Evening!" I say to the sea of heads.

"Evening!" The sea of heads reply.

"Christmas is around the corner." I pause. "Literally."

Laughter again.

I fake a yawn. "That work was nothing compared to the work put into this show." I walk over to a lone blue hula-hoop sitting on the center of the stage. This trick always freaks me out. I bend to pick it up, but it swings to the other side of the stage. "Hey! You little sneak. Get over here!"

The hula-hoop stands up and as if a human, shakes its head.

The crowd laughs.

I point to a spot next to me. "Right now, mister!"

The hula-hoop springs into the air and flies over my head and to the other side of the stage.

"Let's not make this hard. Now, please come."

Another shake of the "head." This time it jumps off the stage and rolls up the isle and right to Catalin who stares at me with half amusement and almost a glimmer of anger.

He grabs the hula-hoop and throws it in the air and it flies back to me. I try to catch it, but instead it smacks me in the face.

More laughter.

Before I can look back at Catalin, he manages to come up beside me.

"I hope my assistant has amused you with more than this." He says. "Have you seen the lobby? I mean, stickers on door knobs?"

The crowd laughs.

"Hey, I thought that'd be cute." I mumble.

"Sorry, the stickers are adorable." He says.

More laughter.

"My darling, may I have this dance?" Catalin says, extending his hand to me.

I stick my tongue out at him the way Lucille Ball always did.

The laughter continues.

Catalin grabs my shoulders and pulls me close. Tango like music starts. I am so not ready for this.

We start a slow tango and it feels good to be in his arms, but the fear burns within for I know what is to come.

Once the music stops, so does my heart.

I take a deep breath as Catalin lifts me. As practiced, I lift my legs up and Catalin slowly releases me and steps back. I stay in the air. As the crowd cheers, I take in the feeling of sweet nothingness. All worries have seemingly dissipated. I feel weightless and like I'm on a cloud.

I look down at Catalin who's stuck in concentration. He points his hand at me and as if I were attached by a string, he pulls me forward and I float till I'm hovering over him. He proves that I'm not attached by string and he slowly lowers me down.

The crowd stands in unison and cheer crazily.

I hug Catalin with all my might.

"How do you feel?" He whispers in my ear.

"Amazing." We step back and bow.

After the crowd leaves the theater, we still stand there.

"I'm sorry about the lobby. I —" I start but Catalin cuts me off.

"It's beautiful. Thank you." He says with a smile.

My jaw drops into a fat O.

"That's not lady like." He closes my mouth with his hand. "Thank you for amusing my audience."

"No problem. But that thing is freaky. How does it fly, move . . . ?"

"Magic."

I shake my head. "So how did that meet go?"

He shrugs. "It was all right. He wanted to televise me."

I smile. "Okay. That's a good thing! You could be famous."

"I am in my own way. I'll never be as good as him because he can use computers and television."

"Well, you can kick his ass by doing it yourself."

His blue eyes sway like an ocean. "Unfortunately no."

"But why?"

He says nothing but instead kisses me full on the lips. Just like last week's performance, he has me in a trance. My knees go weak and I cling to him for support. My tongue battles for stability and his seems to battle for sanity.

It seems like an eternity passes before he releases me.

Catalin stares at his feet. "We must . . . Go."

I nod and watch him walk to the lobby. "Oh, snap!"

I hear a familiar giggle. Don emerges from the curtain. "He likes you."

It hits me then. "No, sweetie. He likes the thought of me."

"What does that mean?" He asks.

"Nothing . . ." I rush off the stage and Don trots to keep up with me.

"Tell me, Alessa." Don pleads but silences as we reach the lobby.

"In time you'll understand." It takes a moment for my eyes to adjust. I face Don. "Is my make-up smudged?"

He shakes his head. "All good. I'll meet you at the dining hall."

"Yeah."

Later that night, as Melina tries to teach me the piano, I discover it easy to forget the kiss. I know he only likes the thought of me. I have been here longer than any other assistant and he also has probably been single for years. Why else would he like me? When I mess up a couple keys, Melina stops me.

"What is shuddering your bones?" Melina says.

I shake my head. "Nothing, why?"

"Your tension is throwing knives."

I try to smile. "Sorry. Weird show."

She lets out a *humph* and crosses her arms. "Oh, I'm sure that's the case."

There's a knock at the door and she disappears.

"I wish you would stop doing that!" I yell to the empty room. I walk to the door and open in. When I see Catalin, it takes all of my inner strength to not yell at him.

He keeps his normal elegant posture. Pride. "May I show you my room?"

Did he just say that? "Really?"

His face turns red. "Not like that. No. I have to talk to you."

"What's wrong with here?"

"I have to show you something as well."

"Fine. Let me get my slippers." It is kind of awkward to be wearing blue pajama pants with multiple white snowflakes on it with a navy tee to match it. I go to the bed where my new white slippers sit. Demetrius gave me them after I stepped on a thumb tack with bare feet.

When I enter Catalin's room, I am struck by awe. It's a big open room, lightened with various candles. The main room holds only a pale blue velvet chaise, a coffee table, a book shelf that takes up a whole wall, and a china cabinet that holds various little bottles. Potions?

The smell of musk scented incense fills the room regardless of the fact there is no such thing to be found. I kick off my slippers and let my feet graze the velvety green carpet. I run my hand down the scratchy yet smooth beige and white striped wall. I take a deep breath and notice a slim oak wood door huddled between a wall and the book shelf.

"What's in the room?" I ask Catalin.

Catalin takes three strides and reaches the china cabinet. "My room." He smiles. "Come."

I comply like a puppy and stand beside him. I notice our reflection in the glass. Our reflections are merely a mist, hard to see but there.

He opens the cabinet. There's about seven shelves and five vials on each shelf. Each shelf represents each color of the rainbow. But it is the bottom shelf, the one with purple colors that catches my eye. The center one, the one that pushes the shades of purple from light to dark. It's also heart shaped. It isn't dark nor is it light. It isn't evil nor is it good.

I reach toward the vial only to receive a strong, warning grip on my wrist.

"Out of all of these potions, this is the most dangerous." He warns.

I pull my hand back. "Sorry. What is it?"

He closes the cabinet. "Take a seat." We sit on the blue couch which I find myself sinking into like I'm drowning in a sea of cushion. I curl my legs up and stare at Catalin, awaiting my answer.

He sighs heavily. "That potion can stop your heart beat, it can stop any flow of oxygen. You must never even touch it."

I surprise myself for not being surprised. "How do you know it does that?"

He arches his left eye brow. "Really?"

"I'm serious. If you tried it, it would've killed you."

"Not entirely. I've tried it as a test to see if I can bring myself back from the dead."

"Shucks, it worked."

He laughs. Not his normal, casual laugh. But a full, almost silent laugh. He even hunches over and holds his stomach. I can't help but to laugh along.

Soon, he clears his throat and looks at me. "Clever. Yes, it did work. But I am afraid I don't know how to bring anyone else back from the dead."

"Wait. Once you're dead, you're dead. Right?" I say, thinking out loud, hardly realizing what I said at all.

Catalin seems to fade to a far away place. "I feel as if I can trust you." He barely says, it comes out like a light breath of air.

"I'm sorry. I didn't mean to bring anything up. I should go."

He shakes his head and looks into my eyes. "I want you to know this."

I relax my shoulders and prepare for a story. "I want you to know I'm listening."

"When I was born, the first thing I saw was my dad in his magician uniform." He laughs suddenly, as if remembering a good time. "For Heaven's sake, my mother was his assistant. She went into early delivery while performing. Ironically, my dad was trying to pull a rabbit out of a hat. Instead, he got me but not out of a hat."

I can't help but to chuckle.

"I grew up in this hotel." He continues. "I loved running around and driving old Demetrius out of hit wits. He never gave up on me. He knew I would grow in to something more than this hotel. I guess I never did. My mother passed away from cancer while I went off to college and soon my father grew ill. I was just shy of turning twenty five when I decided I needed to take the hotel over. I performed so many shows just to keep the heart of this place beating. Demetrius tried to tell me my father would have been proud. I feel like I have been so selfish."

I try to become a sponge to absorb that story. "Catalin, I'm so sorry. It's got to be so hard. But you are not selfish. This hotel is amazing. I'm sure your father would be proud."

"Thank you, but I can not agree."

❧Chapter Six☙

The following day I wake up too early. Four in the morning keeps a thin veil over the city as it nears the time to truly awaken. I lie in my bed and stare at the ceiling but not really staring at it. I think of the times with my own mother. How precious those moments are. I never really had any times with my father besides my birth. I remember my mother crying every single time I cried. I remember when I fell off a swing and scraped my knee, I refrained from crying so my mother wouldn't cry. I remember the late nights with a babysitter. She would tell me my mother was working late. But I knew better.

I knew my mother got out of work early to go on a date that would last until the midnight hour. She would come home, pay the sitter with a wad of cash and go straight to bed. I remember tucking her in and taking her high heels off each time.

I try to imagine a little Catalin and what he must have been like as a boy. He must have had those chubby red cheeks. I can picture him sprinting through the hotel and purposely bothering Demetrius. I can picture him standing on one of those luggage racks and going skate boarding through the lobby.

I giggle at the thought, slicing the silence in half, which seems to allow a single stream of dawning sunlight to peak through my window.

Normally, I would get up, but I just turn over and look at the piano.

My mother yearned for me to have some sort of talent. She never gave me lessons but gave me a little key board. That key board became my medication when ill. I learned how to play my favorite songs on that and I would sing.

A light bulb flickers on in my head.

I throw the covers back, turn on a light and run over to the piano.

As I start playing the keys to My Immortal by Evanescence, I feel tears soak my dry morning eyes. I let them fall and I let myself laugh. I didn't even realize I had yawned. I continue playing. I open my mouth to sing the words, but I stop myself. I can't even imagine what my voice must be like right now.

I was on the roof of my house on my thirteenth birthday. I was no ordinary teenager, but I was depressed. I sat on the roof and cried with the rain. Once it stopped, I went inside and kidnapped my keyboard and held it hostage with me on the roof. I must of played for hours. My mother thought I was in my room, not the roof. Once she found out, she climbed up with me and watched me play and sing. She smiled so brightly, I could have sworn she was an angel.

"Play forever, my baby. No matter what or who hurts you, keep playing." She said. "The pain will go deep and it will hurt immensely. But keep playing. Your song is beautiful and like no other."

I tear up just thinking of her smile.

"When I see you smile!" I heard my mother singing while she made pancakes in the kitchen one morning. She kept singing that Bad English song over and over.

It wasn't long until I picked up the song and figured out how to make a key board cover of the song. Mommy screamed in delight and I heard the spatula hit the floor and the thudded footsteps of her running toward me. She fell to her knees beside me.

"Sing, Alessa. Sing the song for Mommy." She said.

I smiled at her. "I'm not as good as you. Sing for me." I played the tune and she sang the song. I promised myself I would treasure this moment forever.

Doug; Mommy's first boyfriend that she introduced to me. He was kind of goofy looking. He was a mechanic with balding blond hair. His nose stuck out and kind of twisted at the tip as if he'd been punched. His blue eyes couldn't stay in one place. Once one of them rolled to the side, the other rolled up. God forbid, he smiled, his teeth were so crooked. Mommy said there was something about him. Oh, he was nice and everything, he was just a dork who laughed when you weren't supposed to and got mad when you were supposed to laugh. Luckily, he only lasted a month.

I miss Mommy so much more. I know I cannot contact her because she is a newlywed now. I just wish I could think of how she might react if she knew where I am and what it is I am doing. I wonder if she would know what Catalin really thinks of me.

Keep playing.

The words echo within some part of my throbbing brain. I start My Immortal over and sing along. My singing voice shocks me. Mommy told me I had Amy Lee's voice and whatever song I decided to cover of Amy's, I sang it just like her.

I start the song over, singing softly.

I'm not sure how many hours go by of my playing, but when I finally take a break, my fingertips pulsate and I need to stretch my whole body. I sit on the floor with my legs out straight and I start reaching for my toes.

Before long, Lucille barges through my door and pulls me to my feet.

"Lunch and I want you to help me." She orders. I study her wearing sweats and a big T shirt.

"You never go out like that." I say, chuckling.

"Funny." She smiles. "Change and look a little more decent. Let's go!"

She brings me to the private little dining area where she sings with her jazz band. It's a cute little place, the only lighting in a single light by the bar and the stage lights at the stage which is flat and has a blue velvet backdrop. The dry wall matches the curtain. The smell of cigar smoke and whiskey stains the air here. As I look at the fifteen little white tables with two black chairs on either side, I wonder who comes to listen to her.

"Ain't it dandy?" Lucille says with a smirk. "I love it here. It's so comforting."

"Minus the stench?" I say plugging my nose.

She laughs her husky laugh. "You get used to it."

"What do you need my help with?" I ask, remembering her barging in.

She trots to the stage. "Come here."

I join her on the small stage. "I will not sing for you."

She lets out a soft cackle. "No, my piano player is out for a week. Will you play for me?"

I light up. "I would love to!"

ଈଠChapter Seven ଓଷ

I play no problem for Lucille for a week and assist Catalin. Actually, keeping so busy in the hotel does me justice. By the end of each night, I fall right asleep and am refreshed when I wake up. However, everyone seems to be on edge. It's not like anyone is going to shut down the hotel. There's a new guest every day and we have to add extra seats to the theater at least twice a month. I try to be the tension breaker and remain calm and try to crack a couple jokes, which seems to work slightly.

I nibble on a pretzel stick as Catalin hosts a meeting for all the workers. Every time I crunch, he scowls at me and I just smile.

I crunch again, a little too loud.

"*Fermata!*" Catalin snaps in Italian. Oh, boy, do I know that word well.

I chuckle. "My bad." I pop the last inch of the pretzel in my mouth and suck on it. Lucille even chuckles next to me.

"This is serious." Catalin continues. "The—*He* is not pleased."

"Who isn't?" I interrupt, mouth still full of the pretzel.

A wave of gasps is my reaction.

I notice Catalin's eyes are that dark green again. "You all are dismissed." He turns toward the stage and heads to his office. That's how I know to leave him alone. I'm not sure who the He is, but He must not be nice.

The meeting was mostly a summary of what everyone does in the hotel. Catalin let whoever know if he was happy with them or not. He also seemed to talk in code, which is where he lost me. I have noticed, ever since coming here, there was a mystery or a secret. But I never quite figured it all out. I go about assuming it's a nineteenth century themed hotel and the workers have trained themselves to speak the part as well as dress the part.

Lucille rests her head on my lap, as we sit in her room. She has not shed a tear nor has she said a word. She just rests her head and looks straight out the window. After the meeting, she asked me to come sit with her. Ever since then, I've been waiting for her to explain to me what is going on here. But I haven't gotten any information and it's starting to annoy me.

I decide to break the silence. "Lucille . . ."

At that, she sits up and faces me. "Alessandra . . ."

I smile, but it quickly fades. "What's going on here?" I take a deep breath. "Why was everyone speaking in code?"

Lucille forces a smile. "Don't worry yourself. I've been here for a very long while."

"How long?"

Her smile transforms to a slit. "A while . . ."

"Tell me the truth. No one else will. So why can't you?" My eyes actually start to mist. If the hotel will be closing down, I want to know the truth.

She shakes her head. "I cannot."

"Who is He?"

"Enough, Alessandra. Enough."

I rise. "Good night."

As I head for the door, Lucille suddenly stops me.

"Wait!" She cries. "It's almost midnight!"

"Well, if there is no secret, there's no issue with going out past eleven." I smirk and exit. The halls are dark, pitch black. I rub against the wall and try to lead myself to where I think the elevator is. In seconds, I slam into something cold, almost metallic. It's not the elevator doors, but a single door that leads to the stairs. I open the door and start heading up. My room is two floors above Lucille's and since the staircase is pitch black as well, I sprint up those two floors, trying hard to stop my wild imagination. As I exit the staircase, it seems my floor is even more dark and now I'm disoriented and have no idea where my room is.

I hear faint breathing, almost a low growl. I freeze and hold my breath. Horrid images play on fast forward in my skull. A beast or even worse, a devil-like creature is coming to claim my soul. I just know it.

Suddenly, the lights turn on to dim. Just down the hall, I can make out a dark figure and yellow-black eyes staring right at me.

෨Chapter Eight෭

The dark figure walks closer to me until it reaches about four feet from me. I stumble back and hit the wall. My heart races so hard in my chest, it aches. My brain tries too hard to process what I'm seeing, it throbs. I can't really make out the creature. It's skin is like leather that's been out in the sun, It's head is so rounded, it's inhuman. And those eyes. Yellow eyes and black slits in the middle. The stench coming off the creature is horrid. A mixture between a rotting carcass and old milk.

The creature lets out a little growl. "What are doing here?!" It yells. The voice has a robotic growl to it. No trace of human in this thing at all.

"I-I — I." I stammer. My brain cannot even process this creature, much less process words. Besides, this thing doesn't even want me to speak.

"You understand the consequences, I assume." It growls.

I shake my head. I wonder if he's the secret everyone keeps from me. But why would anyone want to keep this a secret from me? Then it hits me like a ton of bricks. I haven't felt this way since Chris left me.

Betrayal.

Lucille let me walk out of her room, even though she knew what was out there. Even if she did try to stop me, she didn't tell me. I trusted her to tell me everything like I told her everything.

A clawed, cold hand grasps my throat. The creature actually grins, revealing shark-like teeth. Another inhuman quality.

"Release her." A familiar voice rumbles from down the hall. "She is ignorant and not worth your time." Catalin emerges from the dark and comes beside the creature.

"This is the only time I will let this go." The creature growls. "You have one more chance to impress me. If not . . ." The lights go off and the horrid stench fades, informing me the creature is gone. I reach my arms out until I find Catalin's chest. Just like in the movies, I start punching and pounding his chest, beyond anger.

As if I were a child, Catalin lifts me and dangles me over his shoulder and he walks easily back to my lit up room. It takes my eyes a minute to adjust.

I walk over to my bed and start throwing pillows. Mommy always knew when I was really angry; I'd throw pillows.

"Jerk!" I yell as I throw another pillow. "Why didn't you tell me the truth?" I throw my biggest pillow and it smacks him right in the face. He keeps a blank face, but in his eyes I see sorrow. Tears well up in my eyes as I throw the last pillow. Just like Mommy, Catalin waits until all the pillows are off my bed before sitting beside me. He's not Mommy and I walk over to the bay window and look out. My heart is still racing, so I can't sit yet or even think of trying to relax.

The city has finally went to sleep. The streets are bare except for a few parked cars. The street still looks slick from this morning's rain. The street light still changes color, knowing that he must never stop working, just in case. A young woman emerges from an alley and rushes across the street to one of the parked cars. Soon, she takes off. I almost envy her being able to just leave.

"If time were true to me, I'd be dead." Catalin says, still sitting on my bed. I don't look at him, I continue looking out the window. "I cannot even remember the year. By the time my father was ill, I worried about the hotel. I knew I couldn't do it by myself. Cancer ran in my family and I knew I would not be able to wed and have kids before my time." The bed squeaks and I assume he is standing now. In the corner of my eye, I see him start to pace. "I made a deal . . . The hotel would go on pause, so to say." Catalin clears his throat. "In return, I had to keep the hotel running. After every year, any guest that had checked in, their memory of the hotel was erased."

I feel hot tears stream down my cheek. I know what he's saying and I know what's coming, but I'm not sure I'm ready to hear it.

"I didn't realize everyone in the hotel would become immortal. If anyone died during the moment the curse started, their ghosts remains." Catalin's voice cracks. "Lucille . . . Demetrius . . . Everyone . . ." He sighs. "I didn't mean for that to happen. I was desperate . . . Sick . . . I was in mourning. I didn't want to let my father down."

It's then I turn to Catalin, who has fallen to his knees, his head bowed, I can tell he's crying. I rush to his side and cradle his head in my arms. His tears wet my T-shirt and I run my fingers through his hair.

"No one would stay." Catalin chokes out. "I didn't want them to. I worried they would be cursed too. But you . . ." He pulls back and looks into my eyes. His crystal blue eyes are red and weak. "I couldn't let you go. I wanted to keep you." He pushes a strand of hair away from my face and watches it as it falls back into place. "But you never even tried to run."

"I'm stubborn. What can I say?" I joke with a smirk.

Catalin smiles. "But now He wants to rid the world of this hotel."

I shake my head. "Why?"

"It's not that he's bored or anything." He shrugs. "He needs a thrill."

"I'm confused."

"As am I. All I know there is nothing I can do to do please Him. I must face my mistakes. I must ask . . ." He eyes seem to glaze over as if he's going to cry again. "You to leave."

I stand up and pull him to his feet. "Sorry, baby." I smile. "I'm a stubborn little brat. You can't get rid of me that easily."

Catalin smiles, but it's weak. "If he destroys the hotel—"

"Oh, well. I'm here. I never quit." Now it's my turn to kiss him. We haven't kissed since that night that seems so long ago now. And it's a kiss we both so desperately needed.

ॐ Chapter Nine ॐ

We have a month to please Him. He not only expects a dazzling show but He also expects everyone to start fighting. The tension is so thick, I'm surprised no one has started fighting. I'm hoping my throwing pillows at Catalin counts as a fight. Also, I haven't spoken to Lucille yet. Not that I'm mad at her, there's a new employee and she has her eyes set on him.

He's a young guy, almost my age. He has dirty blond hair that he keeps gelled back. He rides a motorcycle and is on the wild side. He's very muscular and can pick Lucille up with his pinky if he wanted to. He's the new bartender in Lucille's little jazz bar. All he had to do was twirl a bottle of tequila, pour it into her favorite square class with a lemon and a lime on the top to win her heart. And he goes by the name Bud.

They've already been inseparable. Bud and Lucille have already been caught eating each other's lips twice and only once had Bud been caught sneaking out of her room in the early morning.

Personally, I've caught him dancing behind the bar, singing Journey ballads with a beer hose as his microphone. When he noticed me, beer sprayed all over his face.

Okay, who am I to judge?

Catalin and I have been a little lovesick as well. At least we can hide in his office and it's not like I'm going to do the all-the-way thing. Mostly, we've been discussing what kind of show we can do by the end of the month. Everything seems so overdone already and nothing seems to "pop" but it doesn't stop us from trying. And one suggestion turned into a comedic episode already.

"What about that hula hoop act?" I asked with a giggle.

Catalin laughed as well at the memory of the hula hoop smacking me in the face. "It is highly amusing."

"Or the tango!" I said, having recalled the levitation stunt. "We could have Bud and Lucille dance as well and a few other couples and when the guys lift the girl, they all levitate!"

Catalin clapped at that. "But that is only one part."

I stared at an old photograph of Catalin's parents. "Ghosts . . ."

"Pardon?"

Just then, a ghostly head popped through the cement walls. "You rang?" The ghost was an old man who died in the pool. While he laughed, I jumped and knocked my glass of wine over and spilled it all over myself. Catalin laughed and it took me a minute to laugh.

Don rushed over with towels and when we calmed down, Catalin started to think.

"What about ghosts?" He asked, remembering my idea.

I shrugged. "They can pop out of no where, scare the audience, make purses levitate. All that jazz."

It was a silly idea, but it was all we could think about. My tango idea is the only thing that survived and is still on The List. It's going to be a special performance that night. A full two hours. But if we can't think of anything special to add with it, it must go in the garbage with the other ideas.

I cuddle with Catalin in his room, on his chaise. I rest my head on his firm chest so I can hear his steady heartbeat and he keeps a strong arm around my back so I don't fall off . . . Again. Soon, he's asleep. I look toward the cabinet and then an idea pops in my head. I slither out of his arms, careful not to wake him up and make my way to the cabinet. I open it and scan the bottles till I found a dark, heart-shaped one. I smile as I slip the bottle into my pocket.

Chapter Ten

Another week goes by and I have not told anyone my idea. Two weeks remain until the big event. Catalin and I are still trying to figure out various ideas. I know I should tell him my idea, but I know he won't allow it. So it'll have to be a surprise. We've come up with one more idea and it's now on The List. We'll start the show with a twenty-five minute tango number and for five more minutes, the ladies will levitate and make different poses in the air. After the levitation, we'll do something similar with the hula hoop idea. Romeo and Juliet will fly around the stage, almost pretending to be Catalin and I. The hula hoop will direct the birds around the stage and the whole theater.

Of course, after that, there is nothing.

Except for my idea.

The day plays on like it normally does, except for the fact it's now Spring, so Lucille and I venture outside. It's warm and bright out. We giggle as we walk down the road, leaving Posto Felice behind us. I learned the name of the hotel only recently. I wasn't that observant when I first walked in. I didn't notice the gold sign over the door. The hotel was named "happy place" because Catalin's father wanted it to be exactly that for guests.

When Lucille and I walk into a small clothing store, my heart drops. I want to dress like her and she wants to dress like me. We are decades apart and she's been twenty four for years. Seeing modern clothes, make her eyes glitter.

"Clothes!" She cheers. She rushes over to the dresses, typically.

I clear my throat. "Lucille. Twenty first century, please."

The cashier looks at me weird. "Do you need help with something?"

I nod. "My friend has a new boyfriend. She needs something a little revealing, but still classy."

The cashier smiles. "I've got just the thing."

Lucille is herded to a dressing room and the cashier, a stylish young lady with a bright smile collects various items of clothing and throw them into Lucille's room. I sit on a pink plastic bench and wait.

"Alessa, your clothes are odd." Lucille says, frustration in her tone. "Where are the buttons? Oh, zippers."

Soon, she steps out, wearing a black ruffle skirt, that slides half-way down her thighs, showing of her beautiful skinny, long legs. A pink flowy shirt hugs her curves and makes her arms look longer.

"That's the outfit for you." I state. "I love it!"

"Really?" Lucille blushes. "Thank you. With high heels, right?"

"Of course!"

She goes back inside and soon comes out wearing something I thought I'd never see her in: distressed Capri jeans that go down to just her knee and she's wearing an aqua tank that's ruffled in the front.

"It's really cute! I never thought I'd see you in jeans." I say honestly.

She smiles. "I'm going to buy these. You're next!"

When I'm herded to the dressing room, the cashier throws me dresses. The first dress is a cute, beach-like dress. It's sunny yellow, layered twice with a thin cotton on the bottom and thicker cotton on the top, it hugs my curves, sits just shy of my knees and the strapless-ness of the dress makes my breasts look bigger.

"Oh, God." I say, looking in the mirror.

"Get out here, sexy girl!" Lucille yells.

"I look weird."

"Don't be modest." Lucille demands.

I step out and she squeals. "Catalin would love it!"

My face burns at that and I jump back into the changing room. My second dress navy and floor length and the strap ties around my neck. I like this one a lot more. I step out and Lucille cheers.

"Very simple and adorable . . . So you." She says truthfully.

"I'll buy just this one." I say, stepping back inside.

"And the sexy one!" I hear the cashier say.

The following day, I wear my new yellow dress with yellow gladiator shoes and Lucille wears her black skirt and pink shirt with strappy black high heels. I pull my hair over my chest to maybe hide my girls a little more, but Lucille keeps pushing my hair back.

"You look beautiful, girly." Lucille insists. "Right, Demetrius?"

Demetrius nods without looking up. When he finally does, his face reddens. "You both look . . . Magnificent."

"Thank you." We say in unison.

Bud comes up behind Lucille and swings her around. They giggle as they walk out of the hotel together.

"Is it too much?" I ask Demetrius. "Lucille made me buy it."

"It's just different for the both of you." He says.

"Where's Catalin?"

"Normal." Demetrius returns to his work.

I turn to leave, but I notice something in the corner of my eye. Not something — someone.

Chapter Eleven

The world seems to freeze around me. I only hear my heart beating in unison with the pounding of my brain. I nervously pull my hair over my chest as I take in the sight of him. Long honey blond hair, longer now than when I last saw him. Grey-ish eyes, a small nose and a big mouth. A slim body that looks too small in contrast with his big head. He's dressed in all black.

My last memory of Chris was our break-up. I was getting ready for my twentieth birthday party. As I was getting lip gloss on, he barged into the bathroom. He wrapped his skinny arms around me and tried to kiss me.

I giggled like any young girl in "love" would. "I just got lip gloss on."

"I love you." He whispered into my ear.

At the party, I wore a silver dress with chrome sparkles over the chest. We danced and drank too much juice. Mommy danced with her boyfriend and everything was fine like sparkling wine. As we got ready to cut the cake, Chris jumped on the stage to make an announcement.

"Hello, ladies and gentleman." He said with a fake Elvis accent. Being funny was part of his charm.

"HI!" Everyone replied and laughter filled the small hall we rented for my party.

"I want to dedicate this speech to my beautiful girlfriend . . . Alessandra." He said softly and sweetly. "Even her name is pretty. Good job, Mom."

More laughter. I glowed up at my boyfriend.

His face grew serious. "But I've found someone else. She's even more beautiful and she has a job."

No one laughed and my heart stopped beating. Mommy looked at me and quickly ran over to me.

"I love you, Alessandra. But this is goodbye. I know, I know. It's your party. But it couldn't wait."

He said. Just then, we all heard a car honk outside and he hopped off the stage, kissed me on my head and left.

Now he stands here before me, smiling as if that night never happened. As if *we* never happened.

"Wow, you look . . . *Amazing.*" He says, stepping closer.

Tears sting my eyes but they don't—won't—fall. I can not shed another tear for this man. "How's the girlfriend?" I say genuinely.

He shrugs. "She's out of the picture now."

"So you thought you could search for me and expect me to just go back to you?" I snap.

Demetrius looks up and quickly exits the lobby.

"I was hoping we could at least try." He says softly.

I shake my head. "I've found someone. He cares. You left me at my own party. Hell, you stood on stage and sung a song about leaving me for someone who's prettier."

He shrugs again. "I'm sorry, Alessandra. It was a mistake."

"It was a mistake for you to come here." A man says from behind me. Catalin comes to my side.

I notice Chris's upper lip twitch. He takes a step closer.

"Are you Christopher?" Catalin starts. "The one who has plagued Alessandra's thoughts for hours?"

Chris smirks. "I'm glad she's thought of me."

Catalin arches a perfect black eyebrow. "Well . . . What's your biggest phobia?"

Oh, no, I think to myself, *this isn't going to be pretty!*

Chris scrunches his face in confusion and he snorts out what sounds like a small laugh. "That's all you got, bastard?"

Catalin smiles but keeps a poker face.

"You're a little freak . . . I see." Chris smiles, probably thinking this will be some simple fight. "Let's do this. Winner gets the girl."

"Deal!" I say way too fast.

I notice Chris cringe only slightly.

"I must ask once again, kind sir." Catalin says. "What is your phobia?"

Chris frowns, but it seems forced. "Losing Alessandra."

Catalin's nose flares out for a second. His poker face comes back and he focuses on Chris, obviously trying to read his mind. I should warn him that he'll only find elevator music or a monkey on a unicycle, but I keep my mouth shut.

Looking around the hotel, I notice we drew a crowd and even some cameras flash. Demetrius rubs his hands, while concentrating on Chris, as if preparing to hold him back. I even notice Don's little head, poking out the theater doors. I lock eyes with a stranger who looks oddly familiar but a name or a picture doesn't pop in my head. Before a second thought, she dissipates into the air.

A sudden scream pulls my attention back to the fight. Little black bugs are crawling around Chris. Spiders, cockroaches, and small beetle-looking things. It's an illusion and the creatures are merely a state of mind. Chris fears bugs more than anything. It's pathetic and I'm glad he dumped me that night, almost four years ago.

"Leave." Catalin barely whispers. "Do not return." Catalin turns and exit's the crowd. Instantly I can tell he's hurt by my lacking to inform him of my last, well, first boyfriend. Frustrated, I scowl at Chris.

"Chris!" I scream silencing him and the crowd. The image of the bugs disappear. "It was an illusion. They weren't really there. Just like when we're together.

You were never really there. All I can say is . . ." My voice starts to crack. "Do you remember the song that played when we first met?"

He gives me a nasty look that I can't really read. "Why the hell would I remember that?"

A wave of gasps is reaction enough for him. He turns to leave.

"Dust In The Wind . . ." I mumble.

Chris leaves and the hotel goes back to normal. I feel Demetrius' eyes on me. He's disappointed. I don't think in me or Chris, but something.

"What's wrong?" I ask him, walking over to the desk.

He shakes his head with a shrug. "He was lying about something."

I arch an eyebrow and tilt my head. "Chris? I guess he has a thing for lying."

"No . . . No." Demetrius gets lost in thought. "He's killed someone."

My jaw drops. "Wait . . . What?!"

Demetrius shakes his head. "I've been around long enough. I learned many tricks. I read his mind like a book. There was nothing but pure black evil in his mind. I've only seen such a mind in a murderer."

I shake my head in disbelief. The familiar stranger. Was she Chris's last girlfriend? Was she murdered or did she just die?

Demetrius shakes his head. "I cannot judge nor can I talk to the police. It's all about evidence and facts now. If I were you, I'd run along to Catalin."

෨Chapter Twelve෫

I rush to Catalin's office only to find he's not there. The thought of Chris killing someone makes me heart ache. Sure, he was horrible at break-ups, but he was a good boyfriend. He was nice and he always held the door open and let me speak first. He never really had a temper.

I remember Catalin did walk straight to the theater and the thought of Chris being a murderer pops back into my head. He couldn't kill Catalin, could he? Catalin is immortal but he's not vulnerable, right? My heart races at morbid thoughts. Mommy always told me to think positively. Catalin could have easily went somewhere else. Ten exact minutes passed since I last saw him.

"He ain't in here, Al." Don says, stepping from the shadows.

"Where then?" I plead.

"That guy is gone." Don assures me.

I let out a sigh of relief. "Where did he go? Is he mad at me?"

Don's shoulders slump. "I don't know where he went, Al. He was mad, all right. I'm not sure if at you or . . ."

"*Or* what?" I plead again.

"I—I have to go." Don steps back into the shadows and I'm left to my own devices again.

Catalin isn't in his room or the dining hall. Demetrius suggested to just give him until tomorrow, but I don't think I can even think of relaxing before knowing his current state. I remember my little trip down to the pool and rush down there.

I find the Hispanic man asleep in a corner. No one has been down here recently. Something in the pool stirs. I look closely in the water, hoping Catalin went for a dip.

I see a dark figure head toward the surface. Before I can see who or what it was, I'm knocked to the ground. The Hispanic man lays half over me, fear in his eyes.

"I told —" He starts.

"Sorry." I cut him off. "I just need to find Catalin."

He stands up and helps me to my feet. "He'd never come down here. Why, what happened?"

"My ex showed up and then he just disappeared."

He laughs. "You're acting like a teenager. He'll be back."

"Sorry again. Take care . . ."

Later that night, Catalin finds me in my room, staring out the bay window. Just like when I was little, I just had to take off for some time to myself. Which is what he probably needed to do.

He hugs me from behind and presses his cheek against the side of my head. He lowers his lips to my ears to whisper, "Missed me?"

"Are you mad at me?" I ask softly.

He turns me around so I can face him — well, his chest, but I look up. "I couldn't be mad at you. You thought about that man long enough for me to know who he was."

My face starts to burn. "You've been reading my mind?"

He breathes out a soft laugh. "Do not worry, I've stopped."

I look back down at his chest. "I'm sorry he showed up."

"Me too. He has a blank mind. Nothing really goes on up there."

I remember what Demetrius said. "Did he kill anyone?"

Catalin looks down at me with a reassuring smile. "A man who cries at the sight of a bug couldn't even harm one."

I sigh for relief. "Thank goodness!"

"What else is on your mind?"

He really is true to his word. "I saw a ghost while Chris was here. She was familiar, but I could not pin point it."

"I meant to get to that. On his way out, he dropped a photograph. I think it was of his recent girlfriend."

I sit down on the bay window, Catalin copies and sits beside me.

"It turns out she died in a car accident." Catalin continues. "She was not drunk and her car ran off a bridge."

"Suicide? And how do you know?"

"I did research. I enjoy going to the library to relax."

I turn my head to look at him. "Is everything going to be okay?"

He doesn't answer, instead he just puts his arm around me and holds me close. The gesture is answer enough.

❦Chapter Thirteen❧

The following night, I sit alone at the jazz lounge, sipping some whiskey, waiting for Lucille to perform. The poisonous syrup burns my throat as it makes its way to my stomach, once there the burn settles to a soothing numb. Seeing Chris has set me off so bad. I don't drink under stress normally, but I really just want the whiskey to burn his memory out of my skull before I lose any ounce of sanity left. Every memory creeps up on me like creatures of the night.

Our first kiss. *My* first kiss.

Our fourth date when I slipped, fell, I cried from embarrassment but he just dried my tears and made me laugh.

Then the party.

I can't call myself stupid enough. I should have known about the other girl. I didn't and my mind decides to try and sort all this out now.

I take another guzzle of the whiskey and Lucille takes the stage. As she sings soft, sweet jazzy melodies, I finally calm down. Bud sits on the chair across from me and watches along.

"She is stunning." He says softly.

I just nod and take my final sip of whiskey. "You never know what you got till it's gone."

He looks at me. "I know what I have. I won't let go . . . Not this time."

I smile, happy to know Lucille won't go through another heartbreak. "Good."

"You miss him?"

I know which him he's referring to. I let myself think for a second before replying. "Nope. I thought I did."

"Say goodbye to those who have left. They won't return, but I'll stay right here." Lucille sings.

"I really don't." I continue. "Ever since coming here, I've changed."

Bud raises his eyebrows with a nod. "Ditto."

"This place really is magical." I say, using emphasis on the "really" to refer to the truth of Posto Felice.

"You know the whole story?" Bud asks.

I nod. "You?"

He nods. "Lucille told me last night. I can't believe this place is going down."

Then it hits me. Hope. "This place isn't going anywhere."

"How can you be sure?"

"You'll see."

"Hey, Alessandra." Lucille calls from the stage. "Come sing with me."

⍟Chapter Fourteen⍟

Five more days until the big show. The rehearsals are
driving everyone to hysterics. Lucille is struggling
with the levitation. She's not used to the cloud nine
feeling and it makes her feel insecure. I'm beyond
used to these feelings. It comes with the job, I guess.
About two times now, she ran off crying. Bud would
just sit there and shrug. Eventually we all get the tango
down, even the poses.

As for Romeo and Juliet.

They're worse than me when it comes to being
stubborn. Eight times we have had to chase them
around the theater.

"I got her!" I screamed one night, standing on one of the theater seats, reaching for Juliet. I grabbed her foot before she slipped from my grasp. I lost my balance and fell to the side, hitting the arm rests on my way down. "That's going to leave a mark!" And it did. A nice big bruise colors my skin from below my arm pit to the top of my hip.

Another night, while Catalin and I were running around the theater for Romeo, Juliet finally got the hint to be nice and she sat on the stage, watching her partner fly around the theater and her owners running like maniacs trying to catch him.

"You go left, I'll go right and up." Catalin ordered. Just then Juliet took off.

"Crap!" I screamed. "I'll try to get her." I rushed toward the bird and grabbed her before she got too high. I brought her back to the cage and soon Romeo flew right passed me into the cage. "Got them!"

Catalin shook his head. "We're going to have to give up on them." He left at that.

Alone in the theater, I attempt to train them again. Looking into their beady black eyes, I try to will them to comply.

"Please guys, we need you. I promise to set you all free after the show." I say to the birds. I open the cage and they fly out and circulate around the stage. I whistle softly and they swoop down to the hula hoop and try to pick it up, but the hula hoop flies across the stage. I whistle again and they chase after it.

Soon the duo are chasing the hula hoop and I can tell they're getting frustrated, just as I get with the thing.

"Come here!" I yell to the hula hoop. It sits up and shakes its head. "Stop that now and come here." It complies and rolls over to me. I pick it up and hold it in the air. Romeo flies first through the hoop and Juliet follows shortly after. "Again!" I yell, throwing the hoop in the air and in a split second, the birds rush through the hoop before it hit's the ground. Romeo and Juliet pick up the hoop with their small talons and fly over me and drop the hoop over my head.

෨Chapter Fifteen෪

The night of the show has finally come. My secret is still kept within the vaults of my brain. I continuously remind myself that this could all go wrong. The thought makes me shudder, but in the end I always wind up saying, "Oh well."

As kids, the only show we ever truly brace ourselves for are the school play or talking to the cute boy in Math who knows the first five numbers of Pi, or presenting our project in English and even then it's just a cute little poster with four index cards explaining the pictures. As we get older, we find ourselves in high school. A grueling four years that zoom by. However, each day is terrifying. Every time you step through the doors is like stepping onto a stage with thousands of people watching you. One false move and you're the comedic act. It's no longer about the cute boy in Math or the innocent poster in English.

It's about you. How you control and present yourself. Act like a fool, you become The Fool. Act trashy and sleep around, you become The Slut. Yet, in high school it seems everyone has mastered the little tricks and they create the greatest illusion of all: The master of disguise . . . Without a plastic mask. Only, people like me see right through them. I see them as The Fool yet people still swoon over their presence.

When I was in elementary (when participating in school plays was the majority of your grade) I was preparing for the star act. I was a pink daisy in the field of white daisies. My school's way of teaching us to be unique and happy for who we are. As Mrs. Lilac (oh, the irony) was applying my last minute make-up, she leaned in real close to me so the other kids wouldn't hear her. She said, "You are unique. You are special. And only you are capable of doing this role. Play this role forever."

At the time her words confused me, but I went on to the stage anyway. My heart went from a rabbit fast beat to a sudden stop. Like when that rabbit realizes a snake is hunting them . . . They just freeze. I stared at all the faces, eyes blinking at me, waiting for me to start.

"Ladies and gentleman!" I said even though it wasn't part of the act. "I present to you the greatest show of all!" At that, their mouths spilled out laughter. The piano teacher was disappointed.

Another thing I learned that night: The show always goes on.

"Are you ready?" Lucille says, stepping into Catalin's office where I hide. She knows she's not allowed, but I doubt she cares. She can read my face like an open book. This book reads, "I'm scared."

"Yes." I take a deep breath and stand up, accidentally knocking the small, wooden folding chair over. It folds together in fetal position as it hits the floor.

"My, oh, my." Lucille shakes her head. "We shouldn't get on that stage looking like . . ."

"Crap." I mumble. I let her fix my make-up and adjust my dress so I can look perfect on the outside, while on the inside, I crumble to ruins.

I should be called Roma.

When I spot Catalin, I rush over to him and try to make him hold me for at least a minute, but he refuses and pushes me back which makes me wince in pain. The bruise is still there and it still hurts.

"Excuse me." He sighs and heads for the stage.

As we levitate in the air, the cloud nine feeling returns. I stare deep into Catalin's eyes, making sure he knows I'm trusting him so he won't let me down . . . Literally.

After the Romeo and Juliet act when the hoop goes right through me, it hits the floor with an audible *clunk* that echoes in the theater and the small beads within the plastic slowly settle, like a small maraca.

The charm that gave life to the hoop has vanished.

Back stage, as the crowd applauses, we all gather in a small circle. They talk about what-ifs and what-to-dos and yet I never really hear them.

"Catalin," Lucille warns. "Stop thinking like that. Who cares if we're all banished and set to die?" Lucille is a machine gun now and the bullets won't stop shooting until she reaches the end of the line. "For God's sake it's *your* fault we're all like this."

I could say something and end the arguing. But words fail me.

Catalin just stands there, poker face staring straight at her or through her.

Lucille shakes her head as Bud tries to hold her back. "It is about time you face your mistakes. Y—You—You've ruined all of our lives." She begins to stutter. These are the words she's been needing to say but has never gathered the courage to do so. As her eyes mist, her eyes shine like diamonds. "I wanted to move on with my life, grow old, have grandchildren. *You* took that away from me. Maybe my next life will be better."

Catalin nods his head, knowing the last bullet was shot. He turns and leaves. All the hope I might have had dissipates. I look straight at Lucille. I have no choice but to reveal my secret now.

"I'm so sorry, Alessa." She says. "But I couldn't. I just couldn't take it anymore."

I put my hand on her shoulder. "I know what I must do. Go find Catalin before . . ."

A whole minute passes before Lucille gives up on waiting for me to finish my sentence. "Before what?"

I rush to the stage where whispers of confusion create a chill in the theater. I clap my hands to get their attention back.

"Is there a doctor in the house?" I yell out. Almost instantly a young man rises from his seat in the front row. "Come up."

He attempts to climb the stage and I help him up. He has graying blond hair that is neatly gelled back. A swanky tux only makes him look richer than he probably is.

"Evening." I say and the crowd laughs. "What is your name and your profession?"

He smiles so perfectly that shows he might be a plastic surgeon. "Doctor Maxim LaBlaq." He answers with a faint accent. Maybe German. But what kind of name is LaBlaq? "I'm a surgeon." He winks and the crowd laughs.

"Okay . . . Well." I try to get my stance back. I pull the small vial out of the small pocket under my breast. The crowd laughs again. "This potion will stop my heart. It is up to you to verify that in fact my heart did stop. The Great Catalin will be the only one who can revive me. Again it is up to you to verify he did so."

Before he can react or Lucille can run over to me, I open the vial and chug the contents. It burns my throat like whiskey and tastes like molasses. First the air in my lungs run out of my throat like wild horses straight out my mouth in one big gasp. My brain stretches and pulls in my head, trying to escape the pain the potion has caused. Then my heart stops.

෴Chapter Sixteen෴

I have had a near-death experience before. Mom and I were vacationing in Greece when I was sixteen, just before I met Chris. I decided to cliff dive. Before the thought came to me, while we were still on the plane, I made a vow to stay away from cliffs. The whole plane ride I was terrified. Any slight turbulence and my seat belt went right back on. When we finally landed, I thanked God for keeping me alive this long. Two days later I had no idea I'd be thanking him again. This time for a guy.

A Greek hottie named Bartholomaios. I struggled to repeat his name when I met him. He was okay with my calling him Bart. We met at the hotel we stayed at. All I had to do was slip on a piece of paper and fall right on my butt to meet him. He instantly helped me to my feet. When brown eyes met brown eyes, I melted. I've heard so many stories of people going to a foreign country and they come back in love. He gave me a tour of the town. He showed me how to milk a goat and make feta cheese. In three days I could have sworn I fell for this guy.

The only catch was that he was married. It was like in *the Crucible.* Poor Abigail fell in love with John who was married. But in her case, she at least got to taste him. I yearned to taste him. I've tried, but he was an honest man. His wife just hated me. I couldn't blame her. I wasn't trying to steal him — well, maybe I was. Looking back on it, I acted very ignorantly, very teenager. I didn't care, I wanted him. One day, Bart's sister-in-law came up with the idea to cliff dive.

"It's so fun!" She cheered with her thick Greek accent. "I do it at least once a week." I hopped on the opportunity to forget about this man but at the same time I wanted to impress him. How hard can it be to jump off a cliff into the water? Sure, I can't really swim, but humans float. I wore my favorite bikini: Pink with black polka dots. Clar (as I called her) and I watched as a group of ten-year-old boys cliff dived.

It looked easy and when they surfaced from the aqua blue water, they laughed.

"It looks like fun!" I stated.

Clar grinned. "But you must be careful. If you jump wrong, you could die."

My heart sank. I was so sure of myself. "I'll be fine."

The boys scurried out of the water as their mother yelled for them to come in.

"Want me to go first?" Clar asked.

I nodded. "Of course." She jumped off the cliff and hit the water elegantly, barely making a splash. I wait for her head to poke up from the water.

She laughs. "The water is great! Come on, Alessa!"

I walked over to the edge of the cliff and looked down. The world spins and the coppery taste of fear tickled my taste buds. I edged a little closer.

"Don't!" Bart yelled, his sudden voice made me jump an inch and I slipped. I was too close to the cliff as I dove down, I hit my head on one of the rocks as I hit the water.

From what I was told, Bart dove down to rescue me. Clar had planned for this to happen to get rid of me. Okay, I may have deserved that but it wasn't like I was going to live in Greece and try to steal him. Damn, I only had four days left there. I spent it in the hospital. Apparently, I was pronounced dead at the scene even though it was only a concussion and loss of blood. People survive that all the time.

Bart stayed by my side mostly to protect me from anyone sneaking in and suffocating me with a pillow. "Why would you do that?" He asked me, his sweet Greek yogurt voice vibrated my ears and put a pain in my heart. I loved someone I couldn't have. He saved me when he probably shouldn't have. I'd be leaving Greece as soon as I got out of the hospital and I'd never return.

"I wanted to impress you." I said weakly, blinking my eyes continuously, trying to stay awake. "I'm such a stupid teenager."

He smiled, revealing partially white teeth that were almost perfect except for his two front teeth that overlapped. "Duh. I just wanted you to get the full on Greek experience. Not fall in love. No, the man you're meant to be with is waiting for you as we speak. He's the lucky man."

"Unlucky, you mean." I fell asleep right after that, only to be woken up an hour later. Concussions make the people around you wake up hourly.

෨Chapter Seventeen☙

The crowd cheers. Someone pants as if panicking. I feel warm hands on my arm and my side. My body is icy cold. The world is still dark, I can't open my eyes but I can hear perfectly. My heart beats so very slow. I'm not breathing and I can't decide if I want to. I don't feel pain; In fact, I feel at peace. I see a distant light through my close eyelids. I know I'm still on the stage.

"Follow my voice . . ." Catalin's muffled voice echoes in my head. "Alessandra . . . Stay with me. Follow my voice. Come about." His voice is soft as a pillow and I sink deeper. His voice continues to grow more and more faint until I can no longer hear it.

Mom used to tell me that everything happens for a reason and nothing ever just happens. It's not a matter of luck or fortune, it's a matter of a script. When we come to this world there is a script written just for us. Each unfortunate event leads to a very fortunate event in the end. Do not blame God, blame the writers. I used to curse these writers day after day. When I met Catalin, sure, he made me cry and wish I had never been born. However, in the end, he opened me up and I bloomed like a magical rose.

I also learned that there is no concept of time that is why we believe it goes by so fast. Time never ends, it merely repeats. We die in 1892 and wake up in 2011. Or we die in 2011 and wake up in 1670. History is ever-changing, we just never realize it. I might not be the only one with this theory, but whoever else has it would not report it. People would just go mad. It's easier to believe that at some point everything comes to end. Pardon me, but there is no end, is there?

"Alessandra . . . Please." Catalin's voice pleads. His voice is hard like a rock and clear like the waterfall hitting it. Air slithers through my nose and makes its way to my lungs. My heart beats faster.

I died in 2011 and woke up in the late eighteenth century.

My eyelids flutter like butterfly wings. My vision is blurry but after a couple blinks, I see Catalin leaning over me. His face is out of place, he looks strained. I've never seen him so out of place. His hair is a mess and loose strands stick to his sweaty forehead.

Doctor LaBlaq comes into view and places a clammy hand to my neck. He stands up. "She's alive!"

The crowd goes wild. I've never heard such loud cheers from them. Catalin seems to collapse under weight. He buries his face into my abdomen and breathes heavily. I yearn to wrap my arms around him but I still cannot get myself to move.

As the theater clears out, the doctor looks down on me.

"That was amazing." He breathes out. He takes a deep breath, struggling to keep his cool. "That was the greatest illusion . . . EVER!" He rushes off the stage and out the door.

Catalin lifts his head, still worn out. "Why?"

I blink twice and force my arm to move so I can touch his face. My lips part so that my words can be heard. "I'm that stupid."

He smiles. "Do I know." I wonder what it is he had to do to bring me back to life or if Dr. LaBlaq tried doing CPR.

How did you do it, how am I alive? What is in the poison? I want to say but all I get out is, "How?"

Catalin kisses my cold forehead softly. "In time, you shall know. Can you stand?" He slowly helps me to my feet. All I feel is dizzy and weightless. This is how a feather must feel as it sheds off a bird in the air and it slowly drifts down to the Earth. Catalin steadies me until I can stand straight.

Lucille looks at me, her face streaked with black. Don stands beside her, fear masks his face and he rushes over to me and wraps his arms around my waist. I stumble back, but Catalin holds me up.

Don looks up at me. "Must you be so stubborn!" He snaps, making everyone, even Catalin crack a smile.

Catalin notices something in the distance. "Everybody, meet us at the hall." Unwillingly, they all slowly slip away, Don being the last to leave. Catalin holds me closer. I soon smell that horrid smell of rotting flesh and old milk. The creature makes it way on to the stage. It growls as he nears us, he stops merely four feet from us.

"Well done." It grins. "I was almost hoping you'd fail. But I am impressed." It growls out.

"I made a deal with you when I was young and naïve." Catalin states. "I am willing to make up for my mistakes."

"Nonsense." It says, raising a clawed hand. "I will end the curse. You will live the rest of your lives normally as you would have done so many years ago."

Catalin is taken aback. "What?"

It growls again. "This is the last of me you shall see." He waves his hand and soon vanishes.

"It's over?" I ask.

Catalin nods weakly, unsure. "I think. But . . ."

"How did you do it, Catalin?" I say clearly.

"Love." He breathes out. "I just felt my love for you and I believed in it."

I roll my eyes. "That doesn't bring someone back from the dead."

He looks down at me. *"Il mio amore* . . . That is how I designed the potion. Why else was it heart-shaped?"

My mouth drops in a big fat O. "Catalin, I—" He silences me with a deep kiss filled with such passion, I actually tear up. Even after watching Disney Princess movies over and over, I never thought anyone could love another that much until now. I cling to him for support, but even Catalin is starting to fall over.

❧Chapter Eighteen☙

The dining hall comes to life as Catalin and I enter. Row after row of tables, people stand and applaud. The majority of the population in the hall are the ones who have been stuck in this hotel since the curse was laid upon it. The rest are all guests who most likely went along with what everyone was doing. What I thought was a simple act, turned out to be the greatest gift these people wanted. I came here, afraid, ignorant, but determined.

Years ago, these people came here, with a similar mindset to mine. They wanted to work and get somewhere in life. The only thing they were braced for was working, living in this hotel maybe even get drunk but maybe one day being able to put the hotel behind them while they raise their children and later on the grandchildren. They had no idea they chose the wrong hotel and they'd have to wait almost a hundred years for a stubborn, young girl to break the curse.

Well, I had no clue there was a curse. I thought the hotel was vacant. Now I stand here with hundreds of people applauding me and finally forgiving Catalin. Saying I feel good is an understatement. I feel bliss . . . More than that . . . Contentment . . . The sudden realization that everything *will* be okay. I used to wonder what came before that *happily ever after* but now I do. The specifics don't really matter. What matters is the princess finally feels that contentment and she knows everything will be okay. It doesn't hurt that for once I feel like a princess.

Like Snow White. I took a poison and if it wasn't for my true love, I'd be gone. We all have our evil stepmothers and a huntsmen, but we always have our seven dwarfs and prince charming. What I'm trying to say is that there are horrible people that try to break you down, but there is always someone there, somewhere who wants to pick up the pieces and keep you safe.

"I am gratefully sorry, Catalin." Lucille says, hugging Catalin close.

"No need to apologize. I am the one who should apologize. But in a way, it's good that it happened." Catalin says, mostly to assure himself.

Lucille laughs. A real laugh that no longer seems to carry with it the weight of her pain.

As I look at the ones who've been in my company for the past few months, Damien, Lucille, Raul, Catalin, and Don, I notice how they finally glow. Their smiles radiate and I almost hate myself for never noticing how none of these people were ever able to truly smile.

I don't even notice I'm crying until Catalin pulls out a tissue from his pocket. I push his hand away.

"I'll be okay." I assure him. I give him my best smile. "I just never . . . Realized . . ."

Catalin's big smile shatters my heart. I even feel the pieces hit the pit of my stomach.

Catalin leads me through the crowd, introducing me to people I don't know and that I won't even remember as I go on to the next person. When I learned about Catalin's past, I understood that he had a lot of years behind him but I still looked at him as if he were really my age, with just twenty five years behind him. I never thought of how many people he actually touched and how he had a place in his heart for all of these people.

❧ Epilogue ☙

I could brag about my life and how great it has been. But I can't. Now with Catalin human again, he gets a cold or a headache and all hell breaks loose. First comes the groaning, then comes the whining, after that . . . Oh, boy. Other than that, I brought him to the beach for the first time. The moment brought tears to my eyes. It was like bringing your first child to the beach for the first time. The way they giggle as the waves crash on the shore. Okay, it's hard to picture a grown man giggling at waves, but it's true. It excited him and it was something he thought he'd never get to see. These are the images we take for granted. But there is always someone who has yet to see it.

We're also married now with a young baby boy. We're still at the hotel, performing every Friday night. After the Resurrection, we have regulars and a bigger crowd. Catalin is compared to Criss Angel so much, that it makes him mad. The truth is they don't compare. Criss has only been around for forty something years whereas Catalin has been around for a hundred years. No one can top that.

When I look back on everything when I get stressed, I mean, all the way back to jumping off a cliff for a man I wasn't really in love with, I assure myself it just isn't that bad. It could be worse, yes, it could be better, but moping around won't make anything better, now will it?

ஐCatalin's Storyனை
1925

Posto Felice has been my life now. I was raised on
magik and illusions. As a young boy, I was unable to
even believe in a real world. Even smiles seem fake.
Especially after the death of my parents, how could I
possibly believe in a real world? In a real world, you
wouldn't lose all that you've cared for and then have
to be left with a horrid choice: Let life win and take
you down or you twist fate and create the greatest
illusion . . .

Cheat death.

I've heard of many people before me cheat death.
In some ways, it would be with death defying stunts.

Another way was to survive some horrible accident or disaster. Or worse, make a deal with the devil.

Once, my father took me to the basement of the hotel. I was very young and I thought of this as an art project or just another stunt. I wrote all the letters of the alphabet on separate pieces of paper as well as separate cards that said YES or NO. We placed the cards in a ring around the table and in the center, placed a rock. A small, smooth river rock. I remember all this in vivid detail. My father then began to chant in Latin which was beyond my knowledge at the time. The table began to shake and jump. We held down the table with one hand, our other hands joined together on the rock.

"Who are you?" My father ordered. There wasn't a response at first until he reiterated his question with more force.

The table shook and seemed to growl. The rock pushed over to the D then to E and it got more violent and forceful as it went to the V, the I, and the L.

"STOP!" I screamed and everything went dead. My father patted my shoulder.

"I hope you have learned your lesson, child." He told me. "The works of the devil are no matters to be messed with." He leaned down to my level and looked at me with a stern. "Do you understand?"

I nodded sharply, but it wasn't enough.

"No matter what happens, my son." He took a deep breath, his breath hot and sticky and smelled of spearmint. "There is no reason to turn to such evil. Do you promise me you never will?"

I only nodded, but never promised.

Now at twenty five, I return to the basement and set up the makeshift Ouija board. Using the same rock, I begin my Latin chant. Tears stream down my face. Not of fear nor of sorrow . . . But of pure rage. I curse the world for taking what I loved and for dooming my own self to such horrid fate. The table jumps to life, rocking back in forth, displaying my rage for me. I place my hand on the smooth rock.

"If you're here . . . ." I whisper. A sharp tickle catches my throat and I start coughing uncontrollably, spitting up blood in the process.

I'm dying and I do not have much time.

The table slows to a soft vibration. The rock pushes back and forth, almost as if measuring it up. Then it

pushes across various letters all too fast. It spells out:
WHAT DO YOU WANT.

"What I want is . . ." I clear my throat. "Help.
Please. I'll do anything to keep this hotel going . . . I
do not want to let my father down . . . Please. I BEG
YOU!"

My final words seem to work. The table flies across
the room, hitting the cold, dark wall. A leg snaps off,
sounding like a stroke of lightning. A single shard
of wood lands at my foot. I start to gag at the strong
stench of rotting carcass as if I've stumbled upon a
wolf's kill from last week. I barely see his face, but I
see his eyes . . . Yellow, a dark gloomy yellow that
reminds me vomit.

"You will be cursed." It growls.

My vision starts to blur and I stumble forward.
"What do I do?"

"Just wait, boy. You will be doomed until
redemption." That is all I hear before darkness takes
over.

"Catalin!" A familiar, sing-song voice chirps overhead.
Suddenly something whips my face. The contact is
sharp and it stings my face. But only for a second.
Usually it lingers . . .

"What . . ." I flutter my eyelids, forcing them to open. I see Lucille first.

She smiles. "You clonked out, buddy! Something strange happened last night. And this morning . . . I stubbed my toe and it doesn't hurt!"

The memory hits me like a ton of brick. "What have I done?!" Panic settles in first. But then relief. If we're going to live forever and never feel pain . . . That's splendid . . . Marvelous . . . Perfect!

Lucille shrugs and pulls me up to a sit. I look around and see I'm still in the basement. "Ouija board?"

I nod, guilty. "Lucille . . . We will live forever! No more pain or agony or no worries of aging!"

I get another slap across the face.

Lucille backs up, her face turns pale white, the fear is obvious in her eyes. She shakes her head, disbelieving.

"Why?" She barely whispers out.

I force myself to stand. "Don't worry. It'll be okay. We'll figure this out." She lets me hold her but only for a moment. The truth is obvious. Everyone who was in the hotel while the curse occurred must know their fate.

The only one to take the news better is Demetrius. He's always been faithful and loyal to my family. What ever absurd mistake we've made, he's been by our side and helped us through. Even now, when I've sentenced everyone to immortality, he is still supportive. Thank the gods for this man.

As I sit on my bed with Demetrius beside me, I bite my lip and pull on a loose string on my pants.

"What are we going to do . . ." Demetrius says weakly, defeated. I've never seen him look so . . . Vulnerable.

I sigh heavily, emphasizing that I already feel guilt. "Apologies are not enough. They are merely words. He told me I am doomed until redemption. Until then, I must make this the most spectacular hotel ever and I must become the greatest illusionist!"

Demetrius looks up at me, his eyes red from strain, from the years of holding back tears. He shakes his head softly. "It doesn't work that way. If you do one thing wrong, we are all sent to Hell. This is nothing you can fix. Someone . . . Some outside source is the solution."

I cringe at the thought. "But, Demetrius . . . That could be years from now. I can't wait for someone to come around and redeem us all."

He looks up at me and a single tear falls. "Catalin, we have forever to wait." His words hit like a bullet and linger like a snake bite. I feel the venom take over my blood and sicken me with pure guilt.

What have I done?

What seems like centuries of time go by. I feel old and tired, even though my body can never truly feel old or tired. I've been through so many assistants, I stopped keeping track. Lana has been here for only a week and all she's done is complain of the nineteenth century feel of the hotel.

"It's the twenty first century and this place is old. We need to make is modern and sexy. Like Criss Angel!" Is something Lana would say daily. Damn this Criss Angel, whoever he is. I'd like to meet him and show him what magic really does to a man. It certainly is not fame, jewels, and women. It's pain, guilt, and insanity.

My temper scares Lana off and I watch her scream, running out of my precious theater. It took me ten years to design this place just right. An extra ten years to get all my stunts perfected. I do not even know what year it is anymore.

I clap and the lights go down to a dark, eerie dim. I stare down at my feet until I hear one of the side doors creak open. Demetrius walks down the aisle, someone, a girl maybe behind him. And damn all the wrongs in the world, she is gorgeous. Her hips and waist shake so elegantly, like a dancer as she walks down the aisle. Her big brown eyes show wisdom and her slim lips are drawn tight in a thin line. Her long hair falls in front of her face and I have to remind myself she is not mine to touch.

I suddenly remember Lana and straighten my back. "A little forewarning would have been nice." I snap, taking pleasure as they both jump slightly. "I do not need another woman to come here, waste my time, and run off like a boy in war!"

To my surprise, she speaks without hesitation, determination glazes her perfectly round eyes. "Pardon me sir." She straightens her back so slightly, I'm sure I'm the only one to notice. "I need this job. I need a sanctuary. I have always had an interest with magic. If you don't mind, can you please give me a chance?"

I stare deep into her eyes and try to get inside her head.

Nothing. I clearly see the passion, the wisdom, and the determination in her eyes and it's enough. It takes me a moment to finally look away.

I stand up. "Very well. Demetrius, show her to her room where she'll stay. We'll start in the morning." I turn away and walk to the door where they entered. As I exit, I release my breath I didn't realize I was holding. If I as much as smelled her . . . I would become an addict. This girl will either be the death of me or the redemption we've all been yearning for.